For Erin, Katie, Gwen, Megan, and Lenore,
who all make excellent buddies but even better friends —S.G.M

To my son, Sergio —A.G.

STERLING CHILDREN'S BOOKS
New York

An Imprint of Sterling Publishing Co., Inc.
1166 Avenue of the Americas
New York, NY 10036

STERLING CHILDREN'S BOOKS and the distinctive Sterling Children's Books logo
are registered trademarks of Sterling Publishing Co., Inc.

ISBN 978-1-4549-1993-3

Library of Congress Cataloging-in-Publication Data
Names: Marsh, Sarah Glenn, author. | Gomez, Ana, 1977- illustrator.
Title: A campfire tale / by Sarah Glenn Marsh ; illustrated by Ana Gomez.
Description: New York, NY : Sterling Publishing Co., Inc., [2017] | Summary:
Everything goes wrong on Dragon's first day at camp, despite his buddy's
efforts to show him a good time, until Dragon has a chance to show what he
does well.
Identifiers: LCCN 2016030675 | ISBN 9781454919933 (book/hc-plc with jacket picture book)
Subjects: | CYAC: Camps–Fiction. | Dragons–Fiction. | Friendship–Fiction.
Classification: LCC PZ7.1.M3727 Cam 2018 | DDC [E]–dc23 LC record available at https://lccn.loc.gov/2016030675

Distributed in Canada by Sterling Publishing Co., Inc.
c/o Canadian Manda Group, 664 Annette Street
Toronto, Ontario M6S 2C8, Canada
Distributed in the United Kingdom by GMC Distribution Services
Castle Place, 166 High Street, Lewes, East Sussex BN7 1XU, England
Distributed in Australia by NewSouth Books, 45 Beach Street, Coogee NSW 2034, Australia

For information about custom editions, special sales, and premium and corporate purchases,
please contact Sterling Special Sales at 800-805-5489 or specialsales@sterlingpublishing.com.

Manufactured in China
Lot #:
2 4 6 8 10 9 7 5 3 1
02/18

sterlingpublishing.com

Cover and interior design by Heather Kelly

A CAMPFIRE TAIL

by Sarah Glenn Marsh

illustrated by Ana Gómez

STERLING CHILDREN'S BOOKS
New York

This year, all campers should bring:

- Water bottle
- Bug spray
- Sunscreen
- Flashlight
- Bathing suit
- Fireproof blanket

Today is Dragon's first day at summer camp.

I was new here last year and remember
how nervous I was when Mom dropped me off,
so I volunteer to be his buddy.

Having Dragon with me every
day this summer will be so cool,
because I can show him around!
I see he's excited, too.

I'll take him to all my favorite camp activities.

Like swimming.

Sailing.

And tug-of-war.

The morning didn't go so well, but after lunch is archery.

And horseback riding.

This year, the counselors have asked us to put on a puppet show for the youngest campers. Dragon wants to help . . .

. . . but it's worse than I could've imagined.

I'm starting to think having Dragon for a buddy isn't cool after all.

Nobody wants him around. And since I'm Dragon's buddy, no one wants me around, either.

Maybe tonight will be better. After all, Dragon's still new here.

Plus, tonight's the first Camp Wildwood moonlight sleepover of the summer.
Maybe Dragon won't want to come. . . .

. . . but he shows up at five o'clock sharp.

I try pitching our tent by myself.

But Dragon insists on helping.

After dinner, we meet in the woods to tell scary stories. Dragon tags along, even though he's been afraid of ghosts ever since his older brother saw one in their castle tower.

I don't think Dragon is having any fun.

I just want to go to bed and forget this bad day, but Dragon sees a spider.
I don't like spiders, so Dragon tries to help . . .

"GET OUT!
GET OUT!"

I yell.

Dragon sniffles, looking toward the woods.

I know it's really just my job to show him around, but Dragon looks like he could use a friend more than a buddy tonight.

"At least you got rid of the spider," I sigh. "Let's just get some sleep."

The next morning, as we get ready to hike back to camp, no one can find Dragon. We search and search, calling his name, but there's no answer.

I hope we find him soon. When we do, I'm going to be the best buddy he could ever imagine!

Soon we're lost deep in the woods, too. There's still no sign of Dragon, but something is growling in the shadows. And it sounds mad. Wherever Dragon is, I hope he's far away from the danger.

I want to tell him I'm sorry for not being a better friend.
And I really don't want to find out what's growling at us.
Now something big and scaly is crashing through the trees!

IT'S DRAGON!

The growling stops. The angry creature is gone.
"You saved us!" the other campers cheer. "You were amazing! You scared that thing away all by yourself!"

Dragon grins and then crouches down so everyone can sit on his back between his wings.

"What else are you good at, besides scaring off bad things?" I ask Dragon as we climb aboard.

It turns out dragons are really good at flying.

And cave exploring.

And marshmallow-roasting.

Best of all, dragons make good buddies—but even better friends!